ACKNOWLEDGEMENTS

First, thank you, God, you gave me everything I have. My life, my skills, the ability to do what I love, and its all just extra compared to knowing you; Every bit of art I make is for your fridge. Speaking of fridge art, thank you Mom and Tristan for supporting and believeing in me. I'm thankful for my career at Disney too, 10 years with Peter Pan taught me a lot about performing and storytelling. Tony Ley, I look up to you as a creator. Eric Sweetman, you were the first to inspire me to do watercolor. Bob Beckett, I woud not be an artist if it weren't for you. Thank you Lon Smart for being an awesome animator and even though you've had a Disney career I could only dream of, thank you for taking time to steal pizza with me and talk about art. Eddie Pittman thanks for being on my podcast and inspiring me with your awesome writing and art. Same to you Peter Raymundo, Tony Piedra, and the Sundy bros. Go buy 3rd Grade Mermaid, The Greatest Adventure, and Pancho Bandito respectively. They're awesome books. James Carbary, I'm so thankful to have you as a mentor and friend. I owe you every bit of business success I've had. Thank you to Orlando SCBWI, your workshops are better than college. Thank you to every teacher and media specialist who has welcomed me into your school, especially Becky Weso, Kristen Haynes, Sandra Young, Elanit Weizman, Elanna Fishbein, Kim Guilarte Gil, Olga Camarena, Victoria Laurrari, and Saili Hernandez. Thank you Ben Gamla, Pinecrest, Somerset, and all of Academica for welcoming me into your schools. Thank you to my 1100 followers on my facebook page; you never like anything I post but you hit that follow button! Thank you Instagram followers; you guys are way more engaged. Thank you to all 60 people who reviewed this book on Amazon. Thank you Stephen Mackey for being a huge encouragement to me. Thank you everyone who bought this book; you're the reason I get to do what I love.

Dinosaur Press Publishing
Text Copyright © 2007 by Timmy Bauer
Illustration Copyright © 2019 by Timmy Bauer

BILLY
THE
DRAGON

an adventure story
by TIMMY BAUER

In the Country of Dragons,
Where the Volcano Grand,
With ashes outpouring,
Rules over the land,

You'll find by a large
Lava lake by a hill
A gruff looking dragon
Named Fire-Breath Bill.

A mean, ugly dragon,
There's no doubting that.
In his dark, scary cave,
He sits grumpy and fat.

Fools they must be,
Three young dragons brave
Who sneaked from their yards
Just to go near this cave.

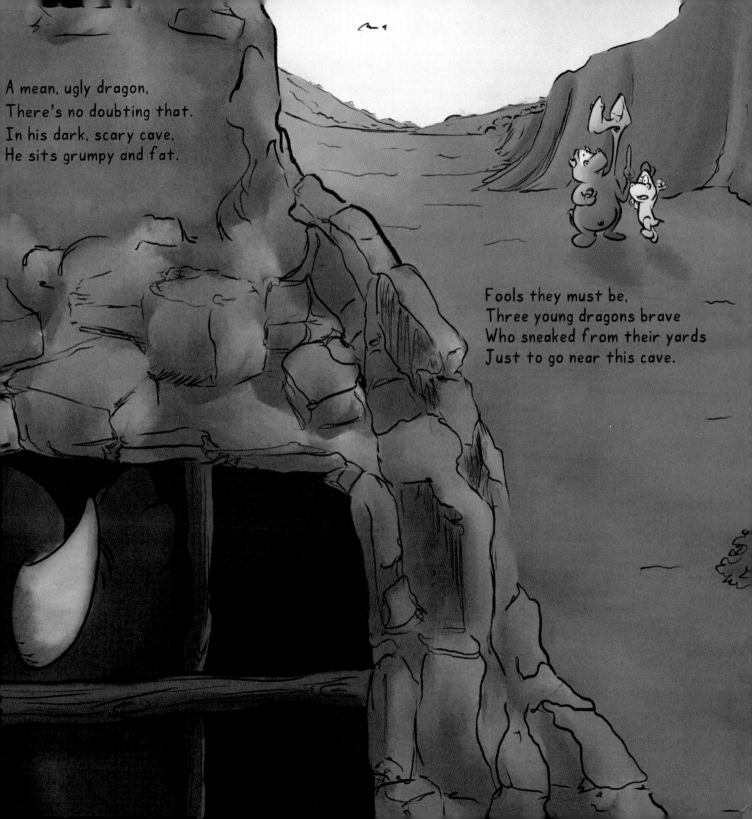

"I heard," said the tall one in low, quiet tones,
"He eats boys like us just to gnaw on our bones!

"You hear of the guy,"
Said small dragon Steve,
"Who wandered alone there
And never did leave?"

"I heard he was roasted!"

"I heard he was toasted!"

"Well I'm not afraid!"
The small dragon boasted.

"Then you can
go first!"

Said Jeffery
and Jim,
Pointing and
staring and
glaring at him.

And with that, they pushed little Stevie up near
The cave while he timidly trembled with fear.

Quietly, quickly, and quaking with quivers,
He stepped to the cave as he shook with the shivers.

But just when he got to the end of the trail,
His four-year-old sister (that loud tattletale)
Yelled from the bushes,

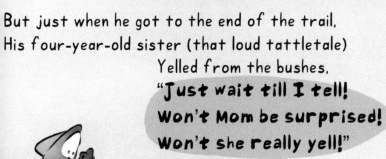

"Just wait till I tell!
Won't Mom be surprised!
Won't she really yell!"

"AH!!!" Steve squealed,
"I don't care if you snitch!
Just be quiet before
Billy hears all of this!"

"It's too late for that!"

A grumpy voice burped.
And they froze in their place.
Their legs wouldn't work.

He glared down at Stevie and Jeffrey and Jim.
Each of them nervously pleading with him.

"Not to be selfish! Not to be rude!
But we don't want to be your next plate of food!
Please, Bill, don't eat us!"

They begged for their booties.

"We're dirty and nasty
and covered with cooties!"

"You want to get sick?!"
They said faking sneezes,
"The measles, the skeasles,
We've all got diseases!"

"Want hair on your eyeballs?"

"Or spots on your toes?"

"Or a three foot long nasty
Green wart on your nose?!"

"Just when you think
That the pain's gone away,
Your brain will just stop!
And you're gone!   ...so they say."

"What have we done?!"

Said Steve when he realized just who didn't run.

"My sister! My sister!
She's still in the cave!

Up off your bum boys!
It's time to be brave!"

"Volcano!"

Steve shouted,
Above all the noise.

The noisy volcano
Shot fiery spurts.
They crashed to the ground
In large flaming bursts.

"We'll never get out!"

Jim cried through the rubble.

"We've got to!"

Steve answered,

"My sister's
In trouble!"

Then Jeffrey, the strong,
Grabbed a piece of a tree
To use as a shield.
There was room for all three.

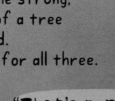

"That's perfect!"
Steve shouted,
"Now back to the cave!"

And off they went marching,
His sister to save.

They raced through the lava
That fell all around,
Dodging the flame bursts
They made on the ground.

When reaching the cave,
Steve shouted, "I've got it!
The plan for this rescue
To end what we started."

Then they marched right back up to the cave without fear.
They each wore a frown, a scrunched nose, and a sneer.
"MHMMM!" Checking their throats were thoroughly clear.

They shouted to Billy,

"Get right back out here!"

HE STEPPED FROM HIS CAVE.

AND TO HIS SURPRISE,

CAME A BIG LOUD DISTRACTION

TO LET STEVIE HIDE.

"OOOOOOOOLL!"

Jim shouted.
And he started to dance
Like a crazy gorilla
With ants in his pants.

Just when he did that, Steve dove and took cover,
As two partnered dragon twins danced like no other.

With Billy
distracted,
Steve started
his search.
He hoped that
his sister
Had not yet
been hurt.

He looked in the foyer.
He looked down the hall.
All over the cave
And around every wall.

Till he got to a table
She sat right behind,
And to Stevie's surprise,
Her condition seemed... fine.

"What are you doing?
We've got to get out!
The pot on that stove's
Meant for us two, no doubt.

And look, Zoe, look,
You see all those books?
Who do you think
Billy's planning to cook?"

Then Stevie and Zoe
Climbed out the window
And landed in bushes
That cushioned like pillows.

They hid in those bushes,
Holding their hands,

Hoping the
brothers
Would follow
as planned.

They ran to the window!

And slipped through the bars!

(sort of)

Up next

THE POISONOUS WOODS

An adventure story by Timmy Bauer

Know the moment I finish my next book:
BillytheDragon.com/next

Watch my progress on Instagram
I post EVERYTHING.

Dragon Head Horn

Volcano

That's Timmy

Billy's Cave

little mountains

Listen to his podcast

Big Mountain

Beach